The Little Red Hen

Retold by **Bonnie Dobkin**
Illustrated by **Subhash Vohra**

TeachingStrategies™ • Washington D.C.

For Teaching Strategies, Inc.
Publisher: Larry Bram
Editorial Director: Hilary Parrish Nelson
VP Curriculum and Assessment: Cate Heroman
Product Manager: Kai-leé Berke
Book Development Team: Sherrie Rudick and Jan Greenberg
Project Manager: Jo A. Wilson

For Q2AMedia
Editorial Director: Bonnie Dobkin
Editor and Curriculum Adviser: Suzanne Barchers
Program Manager: Gayatri Singh
Creative Director: Simmi Sikka
Project Manager: Santosh Vasudevan
Illustrator: Subhash Vohra
Designers: Neha Kaul & Ritu Chopra

Teaching Strategies, Inc.
P.O. Box 42243
Washington, DC 20015
www.TeachingStrategies.com

ISBN: 978-1-60617-129-5

Library of Congress Cataloging-in-Publication Data
Dobkin, Bonnie.
  The little red hen / retold by Bonnie Dobkin ; illustrated by Subhash Vohra.
      p. cm.
  Summary: The little red hen finds none of the lazy barnyard animals willing to help her plant, harvest, or grind wheat into flour, but all are eager to eat the bread she makes from it.
  ISBN 978-1-60617-129-5
  [1. Folklore.] I. Vohra, Subhash, ill. II. Title.
  PZ8.1.D674Lit 2010
  398.2--dc22
  [E]
                          2009037228

CPSIA tracking label information:
RR Donnelley, Shenzhen, China
Date of Production: March 2012
Cohort: Batch 2

Printed and bound in China

  3 4 5 6 7 8 9 10   15 14 13 12
     Printing   Year Printed

Once upon a time, there were four friends who lived together in a barnyard.

A Goose.

A Dog.

And a Little Red Hen.

A Cat.

The Dog was a lively pup who liked to play all day. "After all," he said, "who will chase balls and do tricks if I don't?"

The Cat was a handsome animal who liked to groom himself. "After all," he said, "who will take care of my good looks if I don't?"

The Goose was a talkative bird who liked to gossip. "After all," she said, "who will share the news of the day if I don't?"

And the Little Red Hen? She just liked to figure out what needed doing—and do it.

One day, the four friends decided to move together to a cozy cottage near the river. They were very happy there.

The Dog played all day in their big front yard. The Goose waddled to the farmyard each morning and always came back with new stories to share.

The Cat washed himself on the sunny windowsill.

And the Little Red Hen?
She cleaned the house, worked in the garden, cooked the food, and did whatever else needed doing.

One afternoon, the Little Red Hen swept out the shed and found a bag of wheat seeds. Excited, she brought the bag back to the cottage.

"Look what I've found!" she said.

"Who will help me plant these seeds so that we can have wheat to bake some bread?"

"**Not I**," said the Dog. "I have to play with my stick today."

"**Not I**," said the Cat. "I have to groom my fur today."

"**Not I**," said the Goose. "I have to talk to the cow today. She has news about the goat."

"All right," said the Little Red Hen.
"Then I'll plant the seeds myself."

And she did.

She hoed the ground

and planted the seeds

and watered them well

and pulled the weeds.

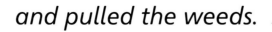

Soon a fine patch of wheat was growing tall in the sunlight.

"The wheat is ready for harvest," said the Little Red Hen. "Who will help me harvest it?"

"**Not I**," said the Dog. "I have to bury my bone today."

"**Not I**," said the Cat. "I have to smooth my whiskers today."

"**Not I**," said the Goose. "I have to visit the pig today. He says there's a scandal with the sheep!"

"All right," said the Little Red Hen.
"Then I'll harvest the wheat myself."

And she did.

She cut the wheat, then gathered and tied
it up in bundles she stacked outside.

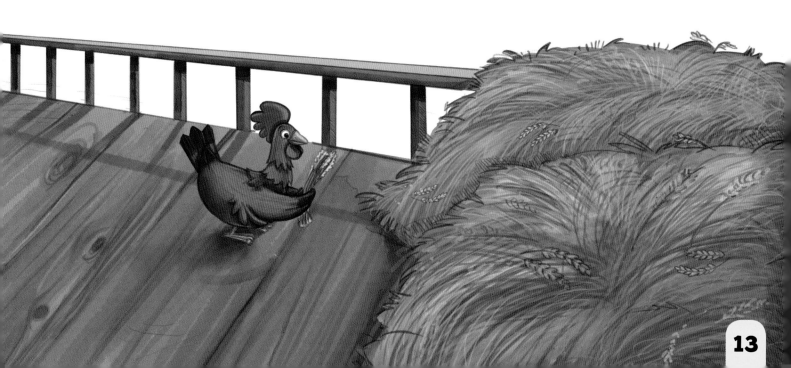

"Now the wheat must be ground into flour," said the Little Red Hen. "Who will help me pull the wagon to the miller?"

"**Not I**," said the Dog. "Today is the day I chase rabbits."

"**Not I**," said the Cat. "Today is the day I clean between my toes."

"**Not I**," said the Goose. "Today is the day the goat said he'd tell me a secret about the cow."

"All right," said the Little Red Hen.
"Then I'll pull the wagon myself."

And she did.

*She cleaned the wagon
and loaded the wheat
and went to the miller's,
down the street.*

The next morning, the Little Red Hen was ready to bake.

"Who will help me make the dough?" she asked.

"**Not I**," said the Dog. "I'm busy chasing my tail."

"**Not I**," said the Goose. "The dust might make it hard for me to talk."

"**Not I**," said the Cat. "The flour would muss my clean fur."

"All right," sighed the Little Red Hen.
"then I'll make the dough myself."

And she did.

*She gathered up eggs, milk, yeast, and flour
then mixed and kneaded for nearly an hour!*

"Now," said the Little Red Hen, though she already knew the answer. "Who will help me bake the bread?"

"**Not I**," said, the Dog. "It's time for me to take a nap."

"**Not I**," said the Cat. "I really must get my beauty sleep."

"**Not I**," said the Goose. "I absolutely must rest my voice."

"All right," said the Little Red Hen.
"Then I'll bake the bread myself."

And she did.

She built the fire, a difficult chore,
and slid the pan through the oven door.
She cleaned the mess that the baking had made,
and finally went out to rest in the shade.

As the afternoon wore on, the wonderful aroma of baking bread drifted through the cottage. It tickled the noses of the napping Dog, the sleeping Cat, and the resting Goose.

They sniffed.
They smiled.
They opened their eyes.

"What is that heavenly smell?" asked the Goose.

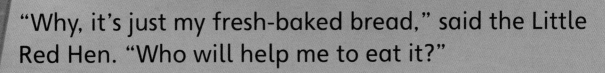

"Why, it's just my fresh-baked bread," said the Little Red Hen. "Who will help me to eat it?"

"**I will!**" said the Dog, jumping up from his rug.

"**I will!**" said the Cat, leaping down from the windowsill.

"**I will!**" screeched the Goose, forgetting to rest her voice.

"You will?" asked the Little Red Hen.
"But you let me do everything else!"

I hoed the ground and planted the seeds
and watered them well and pulled the weeds.
I cut the wheat, then gathered and tied
it up in bundles I stacked outside.

I cleaned the wagon and loaded the wheat
  and went to the miller's, down the street.
I gathered up eggs, milk, yeast, and flour
  then mixed and kneaded for nearly an hour!

I built the fire (a difficult chore)
  and slid the pan through the oven door.
I cleaned the mess that the baking had made,
  and then, only then, did I rest in the shade.

"So do you know what?
I think I'm going to eat
this bread myself!"

And she did!

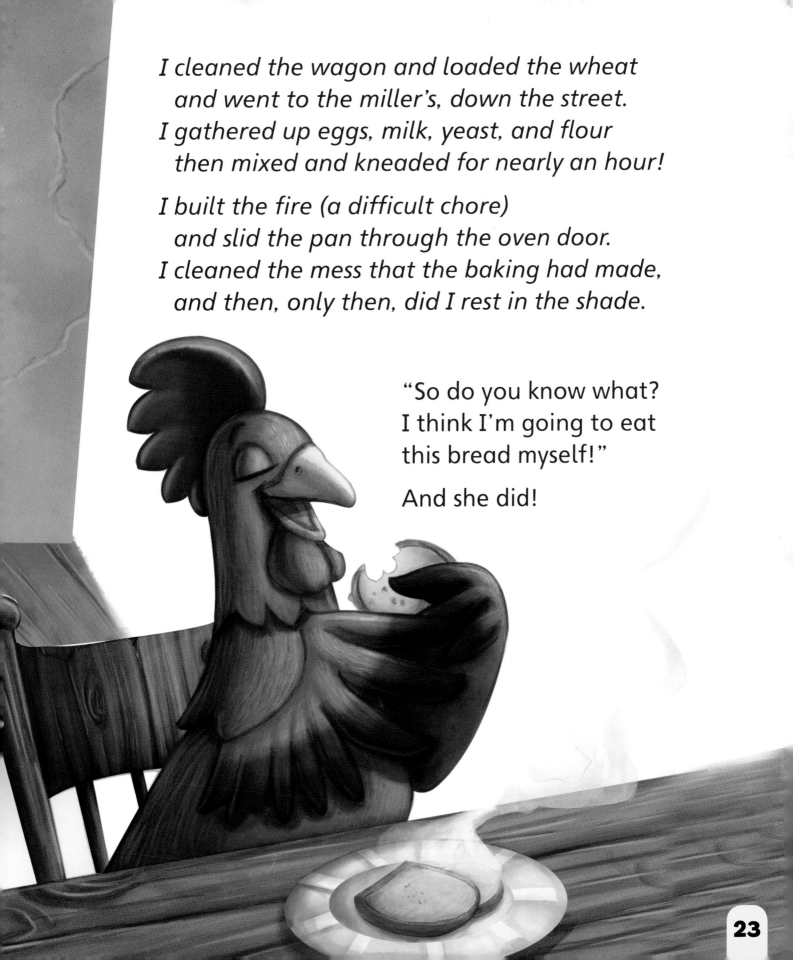

But the next time the Little Red Hen needed help around the house . . .

nobody said, "**Not I!**"